How

Love

FOUND PICASSO

JOSEPH ROBERTS

ISBN 978-1-0980-9619-9 (paperback)
ISBN 978-1-0980-9620-5 (digital)

Christian Faith Publishing, Inc.
832 Park Avenue
Meadville, PA 16335
www.christianfaithpublishing.com

Printed in the United States of America

Opening Credits

Italian music, very upbeat, starts to play with a black screen for just a moment. Credits start rolling as the first scene is of a barn in the Italian countryside during a beautiful sunset. Credits and music continue to roll examining the countryside as it becomes closer to dusk. It becomes completely dark outside, and the barn is shown with a rather large window illuminating light.

With it being dark, you can see the barn light is on with someone burning the midnight oil. The next several shots happen inside of the barn, and we are introduced to an individual whose back is to us—images of a dark-skinned Italian person whose hands, arms, and head are only seen for the first few shots. The individual is working with a paintbrush, vigorously brushing strokes onto a giant canvas. When the music and credits come to a finale, the painting is finished and a still shot of a very handsome and well-built Italian man standing with his back to the camera staring at his finished work of art is admiring his piece. (A cliché stance: he's staring at the painting with his back to us with one hand holding the paint brush on his hip and the other hand holding the palette of paints raised up in the air). As a prop, there is a ladder leaning near the finished painting against a wall while the man is admiring and satisfied with his completed artwork. The canvas is much larger than the man and is dwarfing him in the camera shot where he is standing looking at it. The actual piece of art is wonderful and will maybe from a well-known artist whose art is featured in the movie to help boost the film's popularity?

Scene 1

Knock, knock, knock on the door of the barn the moment after the painting is done with a dark Italian man being interrupted while admiring his art piece. Picasso, who is a very nice-looking Italian man and the artist in the barn (suggestion for an actor, not sure yet?), opens the barn door to a quirky skinny Italian man named Luigi (Adrien Brody type). Picasso and Luigi embrace in the doorway of the barn like long-lost brothers and begin an exciting conversation.

"It feels like I haven't seen you in forever," says Picasso as he welcomes Luigi into the barn.

After a few moments of chatter, Luigi turns his attention to the finished painting, honestly admiring Picasso's brand-new piece of art.

"Do you really like it, Luigi?"

Luigi goes on to encourage Picasso about just how brilliant his artwork is as he strolls around the barn looking at several other portraits of work that Picasso has on display. Picasso follows Luigi around the barn agreeing that he values his own work and even likes most of his pieces. He thanks Luigi and mentions how passionate he is about his art, spending countless hours working very hard on his craft. Yet at the same time, he goes on to share his discouragement on how his name has absolutely cursed his craft. Nobody buys Picasso's paintings for this very reason, and it has literally made Picasso into the starving artist that he is. Living in a barn that his parents' left behind after they passed away affirms such an assessment of being a starving artist.

"With a name like Picasso, who would want to buy artwork from a fraud like me?" says Picasso.

"What's really wrong, Picasso?" asks Luigi.

Picasso also eventually opens up to Luigi about the sorrow of being single and lonely. He mentions how there are no good women around (a flashback scene of two chubby Italian farm girls trying to persuade Picasso into having something to do with them, LOL).

All of this pity happens to involve Picasso while it's his birthday, which happens to be the very reason Luigi stops by the barn in the first place. Luigi refuses to let Picasso throw a pity party and immediately opens up a bottle of wine to encourage Picasso, as well as interrupt the pity party. Yet to no avail, Luigi's hope for a quick pick-me-up of his friend is met with opposition. Picasso is still discouraged by his lack of success and his lack of love especially on his birthday. Picasso turns away from Luigi and puts both hands on his hips looking down at the ground.

A come to Jesus talk ensues! Luigi becomes more direct with Picasso, puts his hands on his shoulder, and guides him to a nearby bale of hay to have a heart-to-heart talk with Picasso. Luigi discusses and affirms in their talk just how much he and his wife believe in Picasso and his artwork. Picasso just does not seem to want to budge on his pity party continuously looking down in discouragement. At some point during the conversation, Luigi gets very animated in the form of a Vince Lombardi half-time speech for some comedic relief. He mentions how it's Picasso's birthday, and he's not allowed to be sad on his own birthday! In fact, Luigi mentions how he has one more birthday gift that he wants to give Picasso. In order to bless Picasso in the cause of helping him chase his dream of being a successful artist, Luigi shares with wild excitement about how he and his wife have decided this year's birthday present to Picasso is a plane ticket to Chicago along with paying the entry fee to a very well-known art exhibit showcasing up-and-coming artists! Picasso receives the brochure about the art exhibit showcase in Chicago with disbelief.

Obviously, Picasso is overjoyed! Both Luigi and Picasso celebrate like true Italians over the kindness of this gift, embracing each other full of cheer and jumping up and down. The rather large bottle of wine is reintroduced into the scene (perhaps a very prestigious wine company/bottle to be used for marketing purposes here). As attitudes change for the better, they start to celebrate the night away as the upbeat accordion music from the opening scene kicks back in again. The camera shot goes to back outside of the barn with all its brightness coming from the window, and the two silhouettes of these two dear friends can be seen in the window celebrating and chatting like Italians do.

Scene 2

Scene opens up with "Uncle" Picasso riding with Luigi's family in a large conversion van. Luigi is driving the van with his extremely gorgeous, voluptuous wife sitting shotgun next to him. Picasso is sandwiched somewhere in the back seat of the van between their thirteen children. There is a fun, upbeat conversation in the van on the way to the airport. Luigi's wife (attractive, famous, and intelligent actress perhaps Monica Bellucci?) affirms their belief in Picasso and suggests that she also believes something miraculous will happen while Picasso visits Chicago.

"Chicago is magical," she says!

Pulling up to the curbside of the airport terminal, Luigi and his entire family empty out of the conversion van. They help Picasso get his luggage and several paintings out. Luigi and his entire family then circle around Picasso for a giant Italian family group hug! After the giant goodbye hug from the family, Luigi comes near Picasso and places both his hands on each one of his shoulders.

Staring Picasso face to face, Luigi gives one more encouraging comment, "You're going to do great, my friend. I believe my wife is right. I believe a miracle is going to happen over there."

A heartfelt "Thank you for believing in me, Luigi" ensues from Picasso.

He turns and walks away with a spring in his step right into the airport doors. With all of his paintings, luggage, and, of course, great excitement, Picasso turns around one more time to wave to Luigi and his large family. Cheers from all of the thirteen children are heard.

"We're going to miss you, Uncle Picasso. Bye, Uncle Picasso!"

Scene 3

(Meanwhile, the character of Love is introduced.)

Love's character in the movie is a high-profile downtown Chicago businesswoman. She's in a powerful position within the company. She wears stylish clothes, has a nice penthouse in a high-rise building near Michigan Avenue, etc., although her true personality is not very business like at all. She is a very, very sweet and loyal woman. Very warm. Very well liked. When I think of Love as a person as well as her personality, I think of Natalie Portman.

Introducing Love in the movie is as simple as Love walking out of her personal office and making her way around the office setting, gracefully saying her goodbyes and thank-yous for another week of hard work to all her employees. This is why Love is so well-liked—because she does things like offer blessings and thanks to her office friends and employees.

One of Love's coworkers, in particular, is a close friend who jokes around with Love and says, "So, Love, you have a hot date this weekend?" as Love passes by her desk.

Love responds with a sarcastic "That's hilarious, Pam. I'll see you later tonight" as she walks out the office setting.

Fun weekend music starts playing ("Walking on Sunshine"?) as Love finishes her goodbyes and leaves the tall office building, walking through the sliding doors on the ground level out into downtown Chicago. She catches a taxicab where she personally knows the taxi driver. Vashti is the name of the cab driver who often drives her home. They exchange warm greetings and have a pleasant conversation. Like, normally, with most people, Love makes Vashti feel important and loved. To exemplify Love's sweetness, on the ride home from work, she and Vashti abruptly notice a city biker get hit by a car. Vashti stops the cab at Love's request, and she hops out immediately to check on the biker. After a few moments of care and checking on the biker, she hops back into the taxi, and she and Vashti are on their way. Vashti smiles at the sweetness of Love after she hops back into the taxicab and finishes giving her a ride to her high-rise apartment. Love exits the cab and walks into the apartment building.

The camera shot then changes to Love on the phone in her high-rise, changing into more comfortable clothes (no nudity but slightly flaunting the truth that Love is a babe). She starts running around her apartment organizing while confirming plans for the dinner party this evening at her place.

Scene 4

Evening has come, and the main story line picks up same night after the office and apartment scene. Love and a handful of her friends are sitting outside on the deck area of Love's downtown Chicago high-rise having dinner.

As Love and her friends eat, drink, and joke together, the talk eventually takes a turn to Love's non-existent, problematic love life.

"Yeah, Love, what's going on with that reporter you went on a date with a while back?"

Love explains to her friends how she's been done with love for some time now. She doesn't believe in love any longer. Of course, somewhere in the conversation, her friends challenge her thinking. Pam, who is her closest friend (Pam is an African American woman), mentions her parents' long-time happy marriage.

"How long have they been married?" Pam asks.

In the conversation, Pam also makes a point to mention her hippy upbringing (thus the name "Love"). The friends continue to prompt and encourage Love to take another shot at love. After a few moments of concentrating on Love's love life, the night continues, filled with much laughter, fun, hope, and friendship.

After a fun evening, Love sees everyone to the door. She then has a moment pause as she walks out onto the balcony with a glass of wine in her hand. Leaning on the railing and gazing out into the Chicago skyline, she takes some time to self-reflect. Something sentimental and supernatural happens (along the lines of seeing a shooting star or saying a prayer) as a tear streams down her cheek. She wipes her tear, walks off the patio back inside the apartment, and drifts off to bed.

Scene 5

Picasso, riding on the airplane to the United States sitting next to an older gentleman, eventually strikes up a conversation. This person could perhaps speak wisdom or encouragement into Picasso's life about his current travels, life situation, and being a starving artist. A conversation may or may not ensue at this point in the movie (not exactly decided if it needs to happen here). It could just be Picasso sitting on the plane having some reflection time.

Either way, just like in the last scene with Love, which happens to be the same evening as Love's dinner party, Picasso has a sentimental and spiritual moment on the plane as well. As Picasso is looking out of the airplane window, he embraces the cross on his necklace, and he sees the same shooting star that Love did. A tear is shown streaming down Picasso's cheek. Picasso wipes the tear away and then drifts off into a peaceful sleep in the middle of the red-eye flight to United States.

(Shot of a plane entering Chicago skyline as day breaks.)

Picasso is shown hopping into a taxicab at O'Hare International Airport with the stack of his paintings and luggage. With fun music playing and a huge smile on his face, this scene captures Picasso riding in the back seat of the taxicab all around the city of Chicago taking in all the exciting views and well-known landmarks. Cinematographer will capture the artistic aura of Chicago during this cab ride while Picasso is literally sticking his head out of the window excited as can be.

Picasso pulls up to the famous Drake Hotel and unloads his luggage and painting from the back of the cab.

(Perhaps a fun check-in scene at the hotel?)

(Perhaps a fun hotel-room scene of Picasso jumping on the bed and being a goofball?)

Picasso eventually takes a shower and settles in (non-nude scene but slightly flaunting that Picasso is a hunk). Sitting on the bed in his towel, he looks at the vendor ticket for the 2020 Chicago Open Art Gala and realizes that the festivities don't start until later this evening so he has all day to go and discover Chicago for all that its worth—which is a good thing because he just now realizes how fancy the Chicago Open Art Gala is and how he needs to be fitted for a fancy black tuxedo. As well, he gets the opportunity to go check out The Art Institute of Chicago!

Scene 6

(Meanwhile…)

Love wakes up with a renewed sense of vision, clarity, and hope for the day. As she slides her way down her wardrobe, which consists of mostly high-end business outfits (possible marketing plug, designer brand name), she comes across a beautiful sundress (something hippy/classy/sunflower-type print, which she will wear throughout the day and will be important to future scenes and the entire plot of the movie). She stops and stares for a moment at the dress to get a literal feel for it. Love decides to put on the dress, pulling it out of the closet with nervous excitement.

Love leaves her apartment with a bit of timidness because of the dress she is wearing. She stares at herself several times in the mirror etc. Walking toward the door of the apartment when leaving, perhaps she picks up a framed picture of her hippy Jesus-loving parents.

Love starts out her Saturday by walking to the local coffee shop down the street. One more scene to affirm the kindness that Love is known and appreciated for: as she walks into the coffee shop, she is greeted by the several baristas who are working there and who always enjoy Love's kindness just as much as anyone.

Several fun comments and chatter about Love's outfit for the day, "Girl, you are looking on point, oh snap."

Eventually, one barista asks, "So, Love, what will it be, your usual?"

But going on the theme of a renewed and adventurous spirit, Love decides to go with bottled kombucha today instead of coffee. Love receives her drink and on the way out, the entire staff sends her off goodbyes and well wishes! She has a renewed sense of confidence that wearing the flower dress was indeed a good idea.

Scene 7

(During these scenes, Picasso notices Love on three
different occasions. Love is oblivious to the fact. She
somehow manages to slip away each time without
Picasso being able to actually connect with her.)

Scene 7 picks up with Picasso at an old fashioned men's tuxedo shop.
Picasso is standing on a riser with the attendant taking Picasso's mea-
surements for the tuxedo. The conversation and scene is hilarious
as the owner/attendant is an old-school crazy Italian guy who has a
mouth on him (Al Pacino perhaps?). It ends up that the owner/atten-
dant actually has a family from the same village in Italy as Picasso.
Picasso happens to know the owner's family as well, so there ends up
being high-energy cheer built around that coincidence like Italians
would. They laugh and joke about all sorts of things including
Picasso's name being a curse and the fact that he's a starving artist. As
well, the shop owner pokes some manly type fun at Picasso for being
single. ("Flying all the way over to America just for a woman, huh?
Sounds pretty desperate.")

As Picasso and the owner are just having an absolute blast
talking and joking, Picasso is still standing on the riser. As he's staring out of the shop's window still being measured, time suddenly
stops (slow motion walk of Love in front of the tuxedo shop)! Picasso
sees the most beautiful woman he's ever laid eyes on walking past
the shop window. It's Love! Of course, she is in her beautiful flower
dress. Picasso excuses himself, immediately dashing off the riser. In
his excitement, he fumbles around and crashes into a mannequin
and a few other display shelves, eventually falling on the floor. He
gets back up and eventually reaches the front door and rushes out

of the tuxedo shop, hoping to still catch Love in time. At this point, the camera shows that Love is already more than a block away and is turning the corner just as Picasso exits the shop. Picasso makes a chase for Love for a few city blocks, but, when he turns the corner, she is nowhere to be found. Love is shown slipping into the door of a neighborhood boutique just a few moments earlier. Browsing some attire at the boutique, she is oblivious to the fact that Picasso is looking all around the neighborhood for her.

Picasso eventually returns to the tuxedo shop in order to pick up his tuxedo and has some type of dialogue with the shop owner. (Maybe some type of encouragement from the shop owner about Love being worth it and not quitting?)

Scene 8

Not to be disappointed and ruin a perfectly good time in Chicago while on vacation, Picasso goes about his day with a positive vibe and good attitude. His next stop is the Art Institute of Chicago. While at the Art Institute of Chicago, the same scenario happens that happened earlier at the tuxedo shop. Picasso spends some very enjoyable time looking around the institute and is increasingly inspired.

At a certain point, he has an encounter with an older-aged security guard while looking at paintings. I would like someone like Danny DeVito to play this cameo role.

The security guard comes up from behind Picasso while Picasso is staring at an actual Picasso painting and startles him. "That's my favorite piece, you know."

"I'm named after him, you know," says Picasso right back to the security guard.

Another funny scene ensues where the security guard and Picasso are in discussion about various topics concerning art and finding love. The security guard ends up sharing some hysterical stories about some former girlfriends and what he did when trying to pursue them. Picasso then mentions how he saw the most beautiful woman earlier today.

"If she's worth it, you'll go after her," says the security guard.

As they are speaking to each other, Picasso suddenly spots Love again! She is walking along down below on the first level of the art institute. Picasso is on the second floor of the art institute and spots Love in her beautiful flower dress once again. Picasso reacts with much excitement, and just like in the tuxedo shop, Picasso has to cut the conversation abruptly short. He quickly gives the security guard a giant hug and makes a dash for Love.

As Picasso is shown running away, the camera pans back to the security guard and he says with a smile, "She must be worth it."

Picasso is then shown running through the museum; hustling as fast as he can, Picasso gets tangled up with another museum attendant and takes a spill. Love has finished her time at the museum and is making her way to the exit without the knowledge that Picasso is in hot pursuit. This time, even though Picasso misses connecting with Love, he makes it a lot closer than last time which makes the sting twice as bad. Just as he rushes out of the museum and runs down the museum steps, Love steps into a taxicab and drives away. Picasso chases the taxi with a few defeated steps, frantically trying to wave the taxi down.

Perhaps at this point of the movie, Love could have her first confused/subtle/slight intro of Picasso?

The taxi is pulling away, and the taxi driver notices Picasso in the rearview mirror and says under his breath, "Some weird guy is flailing his arms and yelling."

Love notices what the taxi driver says and turns around to look. With a confused look, she notices Picasso from a distance and then turns back around.

Picasso spends a moment of time in disbelief. Still encouraged, Picasso keeps his positive attitude and decides that it's a good idea to head back to the hotel and get ready for the big night ahead at the 2020 Chicago Open Art Gala.

As Picasso exits the cab ride in front of the Drake Hotel, unknowingly, his wallet and passport fall out of his satchel. The cab drives off as Picasso walks into the hotel.

Scene 9

Picasso is in his hotel room getting ready for his big night at the 2020 Chicago Open Art Gala. He's getting into his tuxedo, doing his hair, and spraying cologne on with fun music playing in the background. Picasso is filled with a positive attitude and good vibes as he's moving around and dancing a bit because of his excitement for the night ahead.

Picasso eventually catches a taxi ride to the gala with all his paintings

At the gala, Picasso is welcomed to the expo floor and shown where his vendor booth is. As he starts to set up his paintings, Picasso is notified that the gala will start in an hour. He's encouraged to stay at his booth so he can have dialogues with honored guests. Picasso is all smiles!

<<I could use some creative help with ideas and dialogue with the interactions that Picasso will have with some of the guests who walk by his art stand to take a look at his art. Basically, the interactions are not very warm or kind with such comments and remarks that go along the lines of "Psh, Picasso? More like a second-grade art teacher" or even a camera shot or two of Picasso's vendor booth being completely empty.>>

After several not-so-positive interactions and many overheard negative comments from guests at the gala, Picasso starts to get slightly discouraged. Then the evening changes dramatically! Picasso can't believe his eyes! He spots once again from across the gala the most beautiful woman he has ever laid eyes on! Of course, he sees Love for the third time today! She's elegantly working the room, chatting with various art vendors and important figureheads while occasionally sipping a glass of champagne.

Just at Picasso breaks out of his trance from staring at Love and is about to make the move to finally meet Love for the first time, *BAM!* Picasso is suddenly encountered by a guest at his booth in the form of a little old white-haired woman on a mobile scooter. (This scene is hilarious and will hopefully be played by someone like Betty White.) This scene is open for dialogue but something like "Young man, are you paying attention to me?" or "You know, young man, your art would be a really good for the 2021 AARP Calendar." Basically, Picasso tries every which way to escape the conversation, the countless annoying questions, and rude comments made by the old white-haired woman in the scooter, but he can't find himself to be that rude to the old lady. Even though he's cornered by the old lady, there's an occasional camera shot toward Love showing how Picasso is entirely focused on Love's whereabouts.

After several moments of hilarious dialogue between Picasso and the old white-haired woman, Picasso finally breaks free in order to track down Love. As he starts to make a hard move toward her, he is suddenly stopped dead in his tracks. From a distance, he notices a very handsome, nicely dressed, older gentleman who approaches Love and gives her a long gentle hug. The man then gives Love a kiss on the cheek and on top of that holds both her hands for an extensive amount of time while looking into her eyes (Tom Selleck). Picasso, stopped dead in his tracks, is completely crushed by this presumed encounter of Love's love interest. He hangs his head, turns around, and slowly walks back to his booth. The next camera shot pans into the actual conversation between Love and the older gentleman. The gentleman is actually Love's uncle who hasn't seen Love for a few years (dialogue to ensue). Picasso is crushed.

As the art exhibit comes to an end and the party starts to wind down, Picasso walks slowly out the doors of the almost completely empty venue with his paintings in hand. Sad music starts playing in the background; as he stops, he turns around and takes one last look at the beautiful venue where all went wrong and his dreams were crushed.

Picasso then begins walking the city streets of Chicago while the sad music continues to play. Picasso's very posture is that of devastation. After an unsuccessful art show and perceiving to find out that Love is not available, it then just so happens to start raining on Picasso. As the skies open over Chicago, Picasso walks back to the Drake Hotel with a full dose of discouragement. Picasso has hit his all-time low.

Scene 10

As Picasso returns to his hotel room, he verbalizes out loud to himself that maybe some cheap wine and a good pizza might turn his evening around. He looks into the mini fridge to get a bottle of wine and then makes his way over to the phone to call in a pizza order. In that moment, he discovers that his wallet is missing. It's absolutely nowhere to be found. Picasso is thrown into immediate panic mode and starts looking all around the hotel room frantically. (Perhaps a scene with Picasso checking in at the front desk or calling the taxicab company looking for his lost wallet.) To no avail, the wallet is lost! At this point, Picasso is even more devastated and does what only a logical person would do. He calls his best friend, Luigi.

Comical scene where Picasso is on the phone with Luigi, not only explaining how the gala was an epic failure but also the predicament of his missing ID, passport, and plane tickets! Picasso emphasizes to Luigi how checkout time from the hotel and the departure of his plane are both tomorrow! Luigi, who is back in Italy, is shown sitting on his bed trying to talk to Picasso on the phone while, in the background, his thirteen children are tackling each other, goofing around and also climbing all over Luigi during the conversation. Luigi's beautiful wife is also waiting in anticipation of Luigi getting off the phone as well, maybe twirling the hair of Luigi (LOL). Luigi who is friendly, upbeat, and helpful as ever promises that everything is going to be all right and that he will think of something. In the meantime, Luigi tells Picasso to get some rest and that he will call him first thing in the morning.

The camera shows Picasso's sadness. He lies down in bed, turns off the bedside lamp, and stares at the ceiling. Fade to black.

Scene 11

Scene starts with Picasso still sleeping and lying in bed. The phone rings abruptly, waking him up. It's Luigi, who is upbeat and excited because he believes he has come up with a plan, although it's going to take some type of luck! Luigi goes on to explain that he has a friend in New York who is a shipping captain. If Picasso can somehow make it to New York within three days time when the ship departs, he can hop a ride as a stowaway back to Italy on the ship. Cleary, the discussion is optimistic from Luigi's perspective but very suspicious on Picasso's end.

Picasso makes an argument for his apathy, reaffirming the fact that he doesn't have a wallet, passport, plane ticket, or even his ID. "All I have is my stupid paintings and my luggage, Luigi!"

Much more, he's exclaims how he's not even from this country, nor has he ever here been before! Picasso has a bad attitude. At this point, Luigi being irritated with Picasso's apathy, as well as his lack of confidence, gives it everything he's got to Picasso. All of a sudden, Luigi gives another awesome Vince Lombardi half-time come-to-Jesus speech to his friend! Encouraging him in several ways and challenging him to rise above his circumstances, and especially to stop being a big baby, this speech is a magical movie moment! Picasso has a stunned look on his face as the camera shows him holding the phone frozen and amazed from such an amazing speech.

Eventually, Picasso gathers all his belongings from his hotel room and proceeds to check out of the hotel. (Perhaps there's a scene of kindness between Picasso and the concierge he has befriended the last couple days as they exchange goodbyes?)

Scene 12

At this point, Picasso tries to hide how terrified he is. He steps out of the Drake Hotel with as much bravery and resolves as he can. He decides to face the loud, boisterous, intimidating Chicago streets head on. Having no real plan, he starts to make his way through downtown Chicago. Walking the streets, the camera picks up on all the detriments and intimidations that come with downtown Chicago (loud cars driving, honking horns, thousands of people walking around bumping into each other and into Picasso). After a while of Picasso walking throughout the downtown area, he stops to rest near a flower stand cart. The flower stand cart is right smack dab in front of Love's high-rise building. This is where things start to get very interesting.

Meanwhile, the camera pans all the way up above, scaling the building into Love's apartment window where she is on the phone with her best friend, Pam. Love suggests to Pam that after church today, they should meet up for lunch. Love says goodbye, hangs up the phone, and puts on a light coat. She retrieves her purse and fully reforms back into her professional appearance she is out the door. The camera follows her down the elevator and out into the street.

Below the high-rise down by the flower stand, Picasso is resting and observing passersby when, suddenly, he is arrested in a moment of time. Picasso is confronted with bouquets of sunflowers that a customer just bought right near him. The same sunflowers (or any other flower that might be better for the film?) that were on the print of Love's dress the day before. Picasso is reminded of the beautiful woman that got away from him. Picasso decides to approach the flower stand cart to smell the fragrance of the sunflowers. Several flashback moments of Love in Picasso's mind float around and are seen on the screen.

At this very moment, Love walks out onto the city street of her high-rise and is arrested in time herself. She lays, for the first time, virgin eyes on Picasso. She loses her breathe while her eyes are locked on Picasso as he is smelling the flowers. After a few moments, Love snaps out of her infatuation dream state and returns to the responsible adult that she is. She looks at her watch and decides that it's best to be on time instead of being in love. Clearly affected by the sight of such a handsome man, Love walks away from the flower stand looking back at a moment in time that she just might regret leaving. Love realigns her thinking and continues on her path to church. Picasso who is still smelling the flowers has no idea that Love just passed him by.

Picasso, after his moment of nostalgia and being reminded about his visual experiences with Love, is suddenly inspired. Picasso kneels down to get one of his several paintings that is leaning against the flower stand. He quickly opens up his satchel to retrieve a painting, his oils, and a paintbrush as well. The camera at this point is filming behind Picasso as to not see what he is painting, yet clearly that he is painting and adding to his work. After a moment or two, Picasso steps back from his work and to the delight of his critical nature is pleased about his addition (at this point, the audience is still not shown what Picasso has added to the painting).

At the moment, Picasso steps back from his painting to look from a distance we hear an off-camera remark "Wow, that's a really nice painting. Is it for sale?"

Picasso turns around and to his surprise encounters the attendant of the flower stand cart (cameo by Chevy Chase?). A conversation ensues with Picasso and the flower stand cart attendant. Picasso humbly thanks the flower stand attendant for the nice compliment of his painting. There is plenty of banter from Chevy Chase's character for comedic purposes. Eventually, Picasso explains how he needs to get to New York, and he only has three days to do it. By the time the conversation is over, Picasso and the flower stand attendant broker a deal for Picasso's painting. Picasso is ecstatic. It's his first painting he ever sold!

After exchanging goodbyes and thank-yous, Picasso walks a few steps away from the flower stand. He stops, realizes, and looks at the money he now has in his hand. He's amazed that he just made his first-ever official sale. At that moment, Picasso looks up from the cash in his hand and notices directly across the street a Greyhound bus. Picasso looks back down at the cash in his hand again. Suddenly, a flash of inspiration enters Picasso's mind. Immediately, Picasso picks up all his belongings and takes off across the street. Picasso then approaches the Greyhound bus; he enters the bus and takes a few steps up the stairs to speak to the driver. Picasso asks the driver where the bus is heading.

"Sandusky, Ohio," he replies.

"How much is the bus ticket?" asks Picasso.

"A hundred and twenty-five dollars," replies the driver.

Picasso rushes back down the bus stairs directly to the bus depot counter and buys a ticket for Sandusky, Ohio, with the money he just received from selling his first painting! With great excitement, Picasso picks up his belongings and walks back out into the city sidewalk where the bus is.

He steps out to the side of the bus and shouts across the street to the flower attendant, "I'm off to Sandusky. Thanks again for buying a painting from me!"

Picasso gives one last wave and then walks back up the bus stairs with ticket in hand, settling into his seat with great excitement. The next camera shot is of the bus taking off down the highway and leaving Chicago behind.

Scene 13

Love is sitting during church service. She is seemingly agitated and impatient as she looks at her watch a couple of different times. The priest who is giving a long and boring homily has caught Love looking back at the church doors a few different times. The encounter with Picasso is certainly on her mind. As soon as the service is over, Love rushes out of the church doors and races down the giant church stairs. She starts pacing down the busy Sunday-afternoon Chicago sidewalk back toward her high-rise. There is a sense of urgency in her steps and curiosity in her mind as she walks the several blocks back to her place. As she approaches the high-rise, she's drawn straight to the flower stand. Not knowing what to expect, she arrives at the flower stand to find an amazing surprise. Love's breath is taken away from her once again, and her hand goes over her mouth in amazement. Tears swell up out of her eyes. Love has found her first true sign of love. Leaning up against the flower stand cart is Picasso's painting. To the surprise of the audience, we see how the painting has now included Love. In the painting, Love is seen wearing her beautiful flower dress. As tears stream out of her eyes, the flower attendant eventually approaches her and gives Love a warm embrace as if he knows what just transpired. (At this point, there will be some pivotal dialogue between Love and the flower stand attendant.)

"I bought the painting from some poor sap trying to get to New York."

Many ways the talk could go, but the immediate result is having Love know that Picasso is headed to Sandusky, Ohio, and left on a bus that left several hours ago. No matter the specifics of the conversation, one thing is for certain, this is the beginning of *How Love Found Picasso*. Love dashes back up to her high-rise in order to pack a bag but not before one more hug from the flower stand cart attendant. Love takes her heals off in slight panic mode so she can run fast as she scurries off. The flower stand attendant calls out some last funny or encouraging remarks as Love rushes away.

Scene 14

Greyhound bus entering Sandusky, Ohio, on the highway with images captured of "Welcome to Sandusky" signs or places related to Sandusky. The bus pulls into the bus depot, and Picasso hops off. He gets acclimated to his surroundings and stretches for a few moments and eventually starts walking around. Walking the city sidewalks of Sandusky with his belongings for several blocks, Picasso spots a coffee shop in the distance. He heads for the coffee shop and checks his pockets for the last few dollars he has left over from purchasing the bus ticket. He walks into the coffee shop and sits down for a little while observing the patrons.

After a while, he orders a coffee at the counter and the attendant says, "That will be right out," and Picasso goes back to his spot.

Picasso eventually opens the covering of one of his paintings and decides in his mind that if painting Love into one of his paintings was a good idea in Chicago, then maybe it would be a good idea to do it in Sandusky, Ohio. While Picasso waits for his coffee to be served, he confidently paints the same image of Love wearing her flower dress into this painting as well.

Just as Picasso puts the finishing touches of the image of Love into his painting, he is interrupted by a voice that comes from off screen saying, "Well, isn't that special?"

Picasso suddenly turns around to meet another customer named Richard (David Spade's character from *Tommy Boy*). Again, not exactly sure of all the dialogue in the conversation but at some point before their talk ends, Picasso asks Richard if he really likes the painting.

"Yes, of course. Otherwise, I wouldn't have said anything."

Picasso finds some boldness within and asks Richard if he wants to buy the painting.

Richard replies, "No, thanks. I need to save my money for a sales trip I'm taking to Pittsburgh. I really need to sell some brake pads this week. Anyways, I really have to go now."

"But wait," Picasso says to Richard stopping him before he leaves. "Did you say you're heading to Pittsburgh? I'll make a deal with you. I'll give you this painting for free if I can catch a ride with you to Pittsburgh."

In his snappy, cocky, Richard type of way, he replies, "Mmmm, let me think about it. No! Now, I have to go."

At this point Picasso catches Richard's arm and starts to plead his case about getting to New York and explains the desperate situation that he has found himself in.

One more time from Richard, "Mmmm, let me think about that again. No!"

At this point, Picasso's whole disposition changes to that of one who needs mercy. He practically begs Richard to help him to get to Pittsburgh.

After a moment of thinking it over, Richard finds a soft spot in his heart and agrees to give Picasso a ride to Pittsburgh but says, "But we need to go now, and I don't have time to bring this painting home. Here, give it to me." Richard takes the painting and hangs it on the wall in the coffee shop, takes a step back, looks at it for a moment, and says, "Mmmmm, isn't that special? Now, let's go!"

Picasso quickly gathers all his belongings as he follows Richard out the door of the coffee shop.

As they walk out, Picasso looks back at the hanging painting and says, "Can you just a hang a random painting like that in a coffee shop?"

"Eh," says Richard. "I've practically put the owner's children through college with all the years of coffee drinking I've done here, plus the place needed a little artistic pick-me-up."

The scene ends with Picasso and Richard leaving Sandusky, Ohio, driving down the highway in the same vehicle that Richard and Tommy Boy were driving around on their road trip in the movie *Tommy Boy*.

Scene 15

Meanwhile, Love is shown leaving Chicago driving her vehicle with the Chicago skyline behind her. She then realizes she forgot about her plans with Pam and gets on the phone with her. She lets Pam know she'll be out of town for a few days. Love is a bit inconspicuous about her plans and doesn't give any details to Pam. Love says good-bye to Pam and then turns on some inspiring hippy love song music. She's excited about her journey and has a fun little jam session all by herself as she drives through the Midwest. A beautiful countryside sunset happens on the way to Sandusky, with several short comical scenes of Love being goofy driving throughout the middle of the night with a good musical selection playing.

Eventually, after driving through the night, Love pulls into the town of Sandusky, Ohio, in the wee hours of the morning. She pulls off to the side of the road and puts her seat back into the rest position. She decides to crawl over the driver's seat and curls up in the back seat of her car for a few hours of sleep.

Scene 16

Camera fades from Love falling asleep, curled up under the quaint sunrise while in the back seat of her car to a curled-up Picasso slowly waking up in a hotel room. As he wakes up, he looks to the other side of the room at Richard, who is snoring profusely for a moment of comedic relief. Picasso quietly gathers his belongings, writes a sentimental thank-you note for Richard, and then leaves the hotel room.

As Picasso leaves yet another hotel room with uncertainty in regard to his destiny, his confidence has been restored from the happenings of the last day and a half. With the little bit of money that Picasso has left, he buys a transit pass and decides to make his way around the Pittsburgh area to see what kind of blessings he can find. Unfortunately, on this day in Pittsburgh, mostly due to the rough exterior of folks living there, Picasso is having a very hard time connecting with just about anyone (several camera shots of Picasso in areas of Pittsburgh where he faces rejection trying to speak to residents). In fact, residents are just outright rude to Picasso.

After almost a full day of rejection around the Pittsburgh area, Picasso randomly finds himself in front of Saint Anthony's Chapel. With a moment of consideration, Picasso looks up at the giant cathedral and admires the architecture. Picasso walks into the chapel and goes directly to the front of the church and sits on a pew enjoying a few moments of silence.

After a few moments of reflection, Picasso, who is sitting with his head bowed praying, suddenly has a hand come upon his shoulder with a "Hello, young man, may I take a seat?"

Looking up, Picasso turns his head around to look at the hand that is placed on his shoulder. Picasso greets the priest (played by

Dennis Miller) by standing up in respect. Picasso welcomes the priest to take a seat, and a conversation ensues.

(This is another area where I would welcome the writing of dialogue between Picasso and the priest. Not exactly sure what all should be included other than an overall general conversation about Picasso's current adventures.)

Of course, at some point, three things happen in the conversation with the priest: One, the conversation is filled with laughs and lightheartedness (because of Dennis Miller). Two, Picasso is encouraged to keep on with his adventure as well as his lifelong passion of being a successful artist. "Do you think the real Picasso was wealthy and famous over the course of his life?" Three, Picasso gives a painting to the priest to hang in his office. Picasso and the priest share a big hug goodbye, and the priest reminds Picasso that he will keep him in his prayers and "ask the Big Fella Upstairs to send his helpers in order to get Picasso to where he needs to be" (prophetic). Picasso leaves the giant cathedral with a new spring in his step, extremely encouraged and excited to finish his journey of getting to New York Harbor.

Scene 17

Love is shown waking up in the back seat of her vehicle in the fetal position with a big yawn and stretch. She slowly opens the door to get out and steps out onto the sidewalk to the pleasant surprise of finding that her car is parked directly in front of a coffee shop. It's the middle of the afternoon. Love gathers a few belongings and makes her way into the coffee shop. Upon entering the coffee shop, Love is super surprised but more excited by the very first thing she sees. She rushes straight to the painting hanging on the wall of the coffee shop that is directly in front of her. Of course, the painting includes her in it wearing her flower dress. As Love stares at the painting for a moment, she gets lost in time (perhaps a flashback of seeing Picasso smelling the flowers at the flower stand). A tear eventually comes to her eye because she is now fully convinced and affirmed that Picasso does know who she is and does love her.

An abrupt voice saying "So you know Richard as well" comes from behind her. Love turns around to see who has made the comment and meets the eyes of the barista.

A bit confused, Love reiterates, "Richard? No, I don't know who Richard is, but I do know who painted this picture."

The barista responds, "Richard is the owner of the painting. He hung it on the wall yesterday before leaving the coffee shop with another gentleman."

"Another gentleman?" responds Love. "What did this other gentleman look like?"

The barista responds in detail about who Picasso is—"He was super cute, tall, dark, and handsome"—and eventually goes on to share even more information on how both Richard and Picasso are headed to Pittsburgh together. "Something about selling brake pads and a business trip?"

Love immediately puts herself into hustle mode and rushes to the bathroom as she excuses herself from the barista. A comical scene where she is brushing her teeth, putting on deodorant, and trying to put her shoes on at the same time almost falling over while in the restroom. After getting refreshed, Love storms out of the restroom past the coffee shop counter. In synchronicity grabs her cup of coffee and hustles right out the coffee shop door. (Song "Walking on Sunshine" starts playing in the background.) With determination in her eyes, she hops into her car and speeds away (a few camera shots of her driving in the beautiful sunny afternoon while on the highway with the song "Walking on Sunshine" still playing, but not before passing a "Leaving Sandusky" sign on the way out of town).

Scene 18

The very next camera shot has Picasso walking down a Pennsylvania country road (maybe walks by a county sign to indicate where he is in Pennsylvania) in the middle of nowhere on a very hot sunny day. The camera starts behind Picasso with a long view of a country road that stretches on for miles as he carries all his belongings. Picasso is walking alone, hot and sweaty with still a long road ahead of him. While walking along the country road, the scene becomes dramatic at the moment Picasso collapses from heat exhaustion, and time stands still (close-up camera shots of Picasso coming in and out of consciousness, then a few close-up camera shots of a random Amish face or two looking down at Picasso and Picasso hearing some background talking/chatter of these folks who are presumably helping Picasso. (Scene would somewhat be like the scene from *Gladiator* when Russell Crowe's character is left for dead and then picked up by the walking caravan). Then, ultimately, screen fades to dark as Picasso is shown passing out for good).

Scene 19

Love is shown driving her vehicle passing a "Pittsburgh City Limits" sign. She has almost the same experience as Picasso while here. She spends most of the day roaming around Pittsburgh exploring and looking for Picasso with some urgency and no luck at all. All her experiences with the individuals from Pittsburgh are roadblocks and very cold. After searching for most of the day for Picasso, she finds herself discouraged. She sits down on the curb of the street and takes her shoes off for a few moments, rubbing her aching feet. Pondering her dejection of the day for some time, several moments pass. With a touch of sorrow and solitude, Love gets up from the curb. She turns around, and right smack dab in front of her is the same church that Picasso stopped at. Being faith minded, Love decides to enter the church and, just like Picasso, encounters the priest (Dennis Miller). This time though, the priest is standing at the entrance of the church having a cigarette and immediately sees the sorrow on the face of Love. The priest invites Love into her office, and they have a warm conversation. The talk is relatively vague in regard to the specifics of why Love is troubled and in need of encouragement. (During the whole conversation, the cameras are set up looking at the face of each individual while they are speaking. As the camera is looking at Love while she speaks, the audience can see directly behind her. There hanging on the closed office door behind Love, out of Love's sight, is the painting that the priest just received from Picasso. After an encouraging conversation and Love seemingly less emotional than before, the priest gives Love a giant embrace for a few moments. As they separate, the priest walks Love to the office door to open it for her. Love suddenly looks up and sees the painting hanging on the back of the office door. She is all of a sudden ecstatic about the painting and naturally asks the priest a hundred different questions about the painting. Of course, the priest mentions something about Picasso heading to New York and also having to get back home to Italy. Love, for the very first time on this grand adventure, hears the details of Italy in regard to Picasso.

Immediately in her desperation, Love screams out loud with exclamation, "Italy!"

With no time for explanation, Love gives the priest another big hug and hurries out the door.

Scene 20

Close-up shot of Picasso's face, his eyes closed. Then despite Picasso being very groggy, his eyes slowly open. His hands massage his eyes as he's coming to and waking up. In the background, you can hear all the chatter of the Amish caravan. As Picasso slowly rises and looks around, he notices he's in the back of a horse-drawn carriage that he's laying down resting in. There is clearly a sign of confusion on his face, as well as surprise because for the first time, the audience and Picasso see just how big this Amish caravan is (the Amish caravan stretches out like a long parade with about a couple dozen or so horse-drawn carriages with all sorts of animals and people walking next to it).

As Picasso is sitting in the carriage, looking around, he hears a voice from nearby, "Good morning, my friend."

As he looks over, he sees an Amish gentleman walking next to the carriage with a leash in his hand and a goat attached to the end of it. The Amish gentleman introduces himself as Ish (Randy Quaid's character from *Kingpin* who is now older and more mature than his character from *Kingpin*). Ish goes on to explain how the Amish caravan came across Picasso passed out on a country road and in very rough shape. They put him in the back of the carriage in order for him to get some rest and to get out of the blazing sun.

Of course, a conversation (again, would welcome feedback on the dialogue) starts between Picasso and Ish about Picasso's final destination being New York Harbor and having to catch a boat on its way to Italy so he can get home. To Picasso's surprise, that is exactly where Ish states that the Amish caravan is heading in order to deliver a shipment of Amish furniture to a ship headed to Italy. As they are talking, Picasso mentions how he wished he had a cell phone so he could speak with his friend Luigi so he could give him an update on his journey.

Ish says, "Follow me."

Picasso gets out of the horse-drawn carriage and follows Ish for several moments while slamming some water. He follows Ish down the caravan to another horse-drawn carriage. As they are walking to the back of the long caravan, a sign is seen off in the background saying "Welcome to New Jersey." Ish walks up to the last carriage in the caravan which is a covered wagon with a door and unlocks it. Picasso and Ish get into the carriage and a laughable scene ensues. As the carriage door shuts, it goes dark for a moment; and then all of a sudden, the carriage is lit up with red light—darkroom along with images of a command room setting (screens, radar, etc.). All sorts of computer screens and satellite images surround Picasso and Ish. Sitting at the command center, Ish hands Picasso a satellite phone. Picasso has a funny surprised look on his face by this turn of events. Picasso dials Luigi on the satellite phone calling to tell him that he will make the deadline of getting to the ship on time. Luigi is ecstatic! Picasso on the other hand seems a little down in this moment and finally shares his real feelings with Luigi. He shares how he saw an absolutely beautiful and amazing woman who he fell in love with at first sight. Luigi goes on in his typical fashion of being very positive and starts to talk about all the beautiful women in Italy, etc. Picasso has to finally put a stop to Luigi in his excitement and asks Luigi to really listen to his heart, not just the words that are coming out of his mouth. After Luigi settles down, he resets and asks Picasso to start sharing from the very beginning, asking Picasso to share about everything that is wonderful and lovely about Love. Luigi the ever-encouraging friend consoles Picasso in the only the way he can, by listening and being a good friend. The camera fades from Picasso's face as he's speaking about Love right into Love's face who is currently driving across the state of Pennsylvania and also on the phone.

Scene 21

The camera fades into Love's face as she is speaking on the phone with her best friend, Pam (the woman featured earlier in the movie, Love's friend from the office setting and the girls' dinner party scene on Love's roof). The conversation is wild.

Pam says, "What, where are you, woman? Pennsylvania?"

Love says, "I've met someone, Pam, well kind of. Well, it's complicated. I'm in love, Pam."

Pam replies, "What? Met someone? In love? I just saw you on Friday? What is going on, lady? What aren't you telling me?"

Just like in Picasso's conversation, the best friend (Pam) isn't quite hearing her heart, lacks understanding, and is not exactly interested in believing the hype that Love is falling in love. Love has to push back a little bit and asks Pam to please listen to her heart, not just her words.

Pam relents, quiets down, and apologizes to Love, "I'm sorry, Love. All of this is just so sudden. Please start over from the beginning and give me all the juicy details."

Love starts over, talking about Picasso, the flower stand, Sandusky, Pittsburgh, and even New York.

Pam immediately says, "New York, girl, is you crazy?" (comical moment).

Love answers back in a stern voice, "Pam!"

Pam responds back, "I'm sorry, go on," and the conversation ensues with Love talking and talking and talking.

The audio starts to fade, and eventually, the screen fades to a loud city setting and lots of noise—cars beeping, loud talking, etc., but not completely fade of the screen before Love's car is shown quickly zooming past a sign that reads "Ten Miles to New Jersey."

Scene 22

Screen and sound fade into a noisy, big-city street setting; then, several various quick camera shots of the city before the camera shows the biggest production yet of the film: a hilarious scene as the Amish caravan slowly rolls through the Time Square area of New York. The spectacle draws the attention of most New Yorkers who stop and stare in amazement at the traveling Amish circus. The scene then cuts over to Picasso and Ish who are still riding together in the same carriage. Picasso finds a moment to be thankful and sentimental. He decides it's a good time to present Ish one of his paintings (which, of course, has Love in her flower dress inserted into the painting) for all that he has done for Him. Ish seems excited and thankful that he received a painting and gives Picasso a side hug.

He then makes a sentimental remark himself, "We're almost there, buddy. We'll get you home soon. I'll talk to you in a little bit. I'm going to go to the front of the caravan to check on a few things and make sure I put this painting in a safe spot."

Ish steps away from the carriage with the painting in hand and briskly walks toward the front of the caravan away from the command center. All of a sudden, Ish starts to look back from time to time to see if Picasso notices him in a very sneaky fashion. Ish then makes a break for it and rushes away from the caravan and the street in general right into a local art gallery.

Ish is greeted at the art studio door by a haughty art gallery curator (not sure if this will be a cameo or not), partnered with a haughty comment, "Hello, Ish. I see it's your annual furniture delivery to the City".

"Yes, but this time, I have something for you," replies Ish.

He pulls out Picasso's painting to show the curator.

The curator is suddenly caught in amazement about the painting and asks immediately, "Where did you get this? This is absolutely exquisite."

The curator then goes on and on about the details of painting and all its finer points.

As the curator is almost ready to conclude after several moments of description, Ish is shown rolling his eyes with impatience. "...But the attribute that makes the entire painting come together is simply and undeniably the beauty of the woman in the flower dress. How much do you want for it, Ish?"

Ish replies, "Now we're talking. How about $2,000?"

"Sold," replies the curator and immediately grabs the painting from Ish and walks away.

Ish takes out his large billfold, which holds an already large sum of cash, and takes the money from the curator carefully putting the money into it. Upon exiting the art gallery, Ish looks back behind him. With some wonder and a funny look on his face, he notices the curator hanging Picasso's painting in the window of the art gallery with a price tag of $5,000. Ish shakes his head, shrugs his shoulders, and walks briskly up the sidewalk of the Time Square area to catch up with the Amish caravan. He hops onto one of the carriages with much excitement because he just got paid.

Holding onto the carriage like that of a train trolley conductor in San Francisco, Ish yells out loud, "Twenty more minutes to the harbor!" with a giant smile on his face!

Scene 23

Love's car is shown on the highway entering New York City. She zooms past the "New York City Limits" sign with determination in her eyes as she's on the phone with a local airline. Love is asking about any flights that are leaving today out of LaGuardia for Italy. To her surprise, there are no flights that leave for Italy today.

"What do you mean there are no flights leaving for Italy today?"

At this time, the movie starts to have an overall feeling of urgency. Love is hassled with trying to find a parking spot. Now, being directly in the city, she's looking everywhere for a spot to park. Worry starts to take over. Eventually, she finds a spot to park and gets out of her vehicle. Frantically, Love starts roaming the New York City streets looking everywhere for Picasso. Panic starts to set in knowing her time may be up with the degree of difficulty of finding a single individual in this city is nearly impossible. The sights, the sounds, the overwhelming feeling of the empire state along with the sudden disappointment and apparent failure of not finding Picasso finally takes its toll on Love. It's late in the afternoon, and for the first time, the feeling of defeat comes over Love. The weather changes, and suddenly, it starts to rain. Cold, wet, and full of disappointment, Love finds the closest stoop covering and sits on some nearby stairs to get out of the rain. For the first time on this adventure, Love has found real sorrow and has lost all hope. She bows her head into her lap and starts to cry. Out of the rain from the overhanging canopy above, Love takes several moments to embrace her sorrow. Crying is a relief at this moment. After a while, at a certain moment, Love slightly turns her head on her lap.

The camera brings a close-up of Love's face where gentle tears are now slowly streaming down her face and she whispers, "God, what am I supposed to do now?"

At that moment, Love wipes her last few tears away from her face as she tries to regain composure. She gets up off the stoop of the stairs, and as she stands up, she looks directly forward. Like a miracle, directly across the street smack dab in front of her is Picasso's painting! Hanging in the window of the art gallery (gallery lights are shining directly on the painting making the painting look almost heavenly) is Love's instant prayer answered. If Love wasn't crying hard enough before, even more dramatic tears start to stream down Love's face. Tears of joy and amazement start flowing out of her eyes. After a moment or two of being overwhelmed with all the changes of the last ten minutes, Love finds the little bit of composure that she can and makes a dash for the art gallery. As she nears the entrance of the gallery, the haughty art gallery owner is just leaving and about to lock the door. Love being a hot mess with mascara running all over her face and still wet with tears, she startles the gallery owner upon approaching him. The gallery owner takes one look at Love and immediately mistakes her for a crazy New Yorker and tells her to "get lost."

Love protests, "Sir, please, I desperately need to speak to you. It's important." (Not exactly sure of the dialogue here, but the exchange in conversation takes a little bit of time.)

Love has to continue to convince the haughty gallery owner that she is not crazy. The last ditch effort toward the stubborn and arrogant art gallery owner ensues with Love grabbing his hand and comically dragging him over to the painting in the window. Emphatically and literally, Love has to point out to him that the woman in the flower dress is her! The gallery owner pivots his arrogant posture to that of wonder and curiosity staring back and forth from the painting and then to Love. Again, to the painting and then back to Love, who is now obviously wearing the flower dress at this point. In that moment, the gallery owner turns into a believer of Love's story and what she has been mumbling the last several minutes.

With a change toward kindness and a bit of compassion in his face, the gallery owner shares, "Earlier this afternoon, a crazy Amish mobster stopped in with the painting and sold it to me."

As well, the gallery owner goes on to share the key piece of information about how this was Ish's annual pilgrimage to the city, along with details that the caravan is heading over to the shipping docks in order to send their Amish furniture overseas.

"Sir, can you please tell me where the shipping yard is?"

"Sure, it's about a five-minute drive down that street right there. You can't miss it. You'll run right into it."

"Sir, thank you so much. I have to go. I promise. I'll come back some day and explain all of this to you when I'm in a bit more reasonable state. I promise, I'm not crazy."

Love plants a giant kiss on the gallery owner's cheek, completely extinguishing the last bit of arrogance in the man. As Love hustles away, the gallery owner is left standing with a baffled smile.

Love hustles to her car. As she approaches the car, she is thrown one last curve ball on this grand adventure. Her car has been illegally parked, and there just so happens to be a parking boot on it. Love doesn't skip a beat or get discouraged even for a moment. She instantly takes off running down the street that the gallery owner pointed her to.

Scene 24

Meanwhile, Picasso is talking to the captain (not sure who that is yet as an actor, probably another cameo) in the Italian language as they oversee the last few pieces of Amish furniture being loaded into the cargo ship. The captain speaks of Luigi fondly, remembering how they "went to college together and had some crazy days."

Picasso mentions how Luigi now has twelve children.

"Twelve!" says the captain. "He's always been a ladies' man." They both have a good Italian laugh. They continue to finalize the details of Picasso being a stowaway on the ship. After a few moments of talking and some direction from the captain, Picasso asks to use the captain's phone to call Luigi in order to let him know that he is on his way home (melancholy dialogue between Picasso and Luigi where Picasso shares how thankful he is for Luigi's friendship but also how sad he is that this holiday turned into an absolute disaster).

"Still thinking about the girl, my friend?"

"Yes," says Picasso.

"Well, my friend, if it's meant to be, it's meant to be. God knows."

The captain abruptly comes back over to Picasso after checking over the boat and tells Picasso that it's time to ship out.

"I'll talk to you soon, Luigi. I have to go. The boat is about to ship out."

Scene 25

Scene immediately cuts to Love (a close-up shot of her face). She is breathing hard and smiling at the same time. She loves every minute of this chase, running as hard as she can to the shipping yard. Camera pans out to show the rest of Love running down an empty street next to the water and parked boats. Still clothed in her flower dress, Love is running as hard and as fast as she can (some type of upbeat music). (This scene will last several moments, which is the climax of the entire movie.) The camera will keep cutting back and forth between Love running profusely down the shipping yard and the cargo ship almost ready to leave the dock—giant ropes being untied from the dock, anchor up, engine starting (shot of the very same captain in the captain's quarters starting the engine), etc. Then back to Love who is still running. Then back to the ship that has slowly started to leave the dock with a few shots of Picasso.

Scene 26

Love finally reaches the docking station, but it's too late. The ship has left the dock. Love is crushed and completely out of breath as she stares at the ship that has left several moments ago. She tries to yell loud in order to stop the ship frantically waving her arms as well. It's no use. Simultaneously, Picasso has decided to take a walk to the back of the ship to take one last look of America and the New York skyline. As he stands in somberness looking out the back of the ship at the harbor, he, all of sudden, notices a figure on the shoreline dressed in a yellow outfit. Unsure of what he is really seeing, Picasso hurries over to the next closest passenger who has binoculars hanging from his neck and, without asking, uses them while their still attached to his neck (funny moment where passenger is dragged around and very surprised at Picasso). Picasso knows without a doubt who it is on the shoreline! In a moment, Picasso hands the binoculars back to the passenger and makes his way to a nearby railing.

As Picasso climbs the railing almost ready to jump overboard, he turns around to the passenger who he just used the binoculars from and says, "Let the captain know it was meant to be."

Picasso turns and makes his giant leap of faith overboard the ship.

Several moments/shots going back and forth of Love mourning on the harbor dock (maybe a close-up of tears streaming down her face) watching the boat charging away and then back to Picasso swimming as hard as he can back toward the dock.

Eventually, Love finds the composure she needs from such a traumatic moment and turns her back to the sea in order to take on defeat. Just as she turns to walk away, she misses Picasso who reaches the top of the harbor dock after climbing up a nearby ladder out of the water. The timing is impeccable.

Picasso shouts out to Love, "Excuse me, ma'am. I've been looking for Love. Do you know where I can find her?" (Love has her back to Picasso as well as the camera is frozen in her tracks.)

Picasso makes his way over to Love, who is still frozen in her tracks. As her back is still to Picasso, Picasso ever so gently reaches for Love's arm and ever so slowly turns Love around to face him. Love's face has gentle tears streaming down her face as she turns to face Picasso.

Closely, they embrace face to face, and she whispers, "Hi, my name is Love."

"I know," responds Picasso.

"I've been looking for you," says Love.

"I know," says Picasso. "Thank you for finding me."

"Can I kiss you?" whispers Love.

"Forever," says Picasso.

They gently kiss each other for several moments. After the long awaited kiss, Love melts into the warm embrace of Picasso. The camera pans away from Love and Picasso, who have finally found each other and continue to embrace each other under the gentle glow of a full moon above.

The End

About the Author

Joseph Roberts is a forty-one-year-old realist but still dreams of being a professional football player, scuba diver, and running of the bulls champion.

Hailing from the cold confines of northeast Wisconsin, Joseph would prefer to be living somewhere in the Mediterranean than near the frozen tundra of Lambeau Field.

A contractor by trade, Joseph enjoys working outdoors on construction projects such as roofing and cutting down trees, although his real passion in life is being with his friends and family, traveling to exotic destinations, and watching individuals grow in the grace and knowledge of who God inherently made them to be.

Joseph has also successfully raised an eighteen-year-old daughter whose hair has been every color of the rainbow. Her name is Sage, and she has a beautiful soul.

He would like you to enjoy his very first literary masterpiece (romantic comedy), as is it's God's gift to humanity in order to prove that miracles, hope, and especially love all still exist.